Fair and Square

Read more UNICORN and YETI books!

UNICORN and YETI
Fair and Square

written by
Heather Ayris Burnell

art by
Hazel Quintanilla

ACORN™
SCHOLASTIC INC.

For Sean, the fairest agent of them all! — HAB

To Renata, you make me the happiest auntie ever. — HQ

Library of Congress Cataloging-in-Publication Data

Names: Burnell, Heather Ayris, author. | Quintanilla, Hazel, 1982-
illustrator. | Burnell, Heather Ayris. Unicorn and Yeti ; 5.
Title: Fair and square / by Heather Ayris Burnell ; illustrated by Hazel Quintanilla.
Description: First edition. | New York : Acorn/Scholastic Inc., 2021. |
Series: Unicorn and Yeti ; 5 | Summary: Yeti and Unicorn cannot always agree, whether it is about which shape is most pleasing, whose style of painting is best, or, more serious, how to divide up a pie—but the two friends always find a way past their differences, because their friendship is important to both.
Identifiers: LCCN 2020007894 | ISBN 9781338627725 (paperback) |
ISBN 9781338627732 (library binding) | ISBN 9781338627749 (ebook)
Subjects: LCSH: Unicorns—Juvenile fiction. | Yeti—Juvenile fiction. |
Friendship—Juvenile fiction. | Sharing—Juvenile fiction. | Humorous stories. | CYAC: Unicorn—Fiction. | Yeti—Fiction. |
Friendship—Fiction. | Difference (Psychology)—Fiction. | Humorous stories. | LCGFT: Humorous fiction.
Classification: LCC PZ7.B92855 Fai 2021 | DDC [E]—dc23
LC record available at https://lccn.loc.gov/2020007894

10 9 8 7 6 5 4 3 2   21 22 23 24 25

Printed in China   62
First edition, March 2021

Edited by Katie Carella
Book design by Sarah Dvojack

Table of Contents

Shape Up

Yeti stuck icicles into the snow one by one.

Tree. Tree. Tree.

They look like trees.

They **do** look like trees!

They also look like triangles.

They **do** look like triangles!

4

This forest is starting to shape up!

6

I love shapes!

Triangles are my favorite.
Lots of my favorite things are triangles,
like trees and ice cream cones.

Even your horn is a triangle!

Look!
I have a horn like you!

HEHE!

Circles are nice.
Lots of my favorite things are circles,
like the sun and the moon.

12

Stars make me think of magic.

But do you know the shape I love **the most**?

13

14

16

No Fair!

Yeti saw some water.

What are you doing?

18

19

Your painting looks just like what I see.

Mine does not.

Swish!

Swish!
Swish!
Swoosh!

Swish!

Swish!
Swish!
Swoosh!

Swoosh!

Swish!
Swish!
Swoosh!

My snowflakes do not look
like your snowflakes.

That is okay.

But they do not look
like your snowflakes **at all**.

Unicorn and Yeti painted.

And painted.

And painted.

My paintings only look like what we **see**.
Your paintings are fancy.
They look like magic!

I know, let's trade!

39

Half and Half

Unicorn sniffed the air.

What is that good smell?

I baked us something.

What is it?

A pie! I love pie!

Everybody loves pie!

42

44

45

47

YUM!

NOM.
NOM.

49

Mmm.
That was yummy!

Are you done already?

I was **very** hungry.

I cannot eat any more.

50

51

Did your stomach growl?

Yes, it did.

You are still hungry.
You should eat the rest of my pie.

Then I will get more pie than you.
That will not be fair.

You are still hungry, but I am full.
That is not fair.

About the Creators

Heather Ayris Burnell enjoys building all sorts of things. She has built pretend forests — with everything from blocks to sticks and rocks. She has even helped build a real house! Heather lives in Washington State where she

bakes pies as often as she can. But they don't last long because everybody loves pie! Heather is a librarian and the author of the Unicorn and Yeti early reader series.

Hazel Quintanilla lives in Guatemala. Hazel always knew she wanted to be an artist. When she was a kid, she carried a pencil and a notebook everywhere.

Hazel illustrates children's books, magazines, and games! And she has a secret: Unicorn and Yeti remind Hazel of her sister and brother. Her siblings are silly, funny, and quirky — just like Unicorn and Yeti!

YOU CAN DRAW UNICORN'S MAGIC HORN!

1 Draw a circle. Then add a curved line.

2 Add a curved line on the top-right side of the circle. (This will be Unicorn's nose!) Add two legs.

3 Draw a half circle to start Unicorn's mane. Draw one pointy ear. Add lines to make Unicorn's hooves.

4 Draw the rest of Unicorn's mane, connecting it to the bottom tip of the curved half circle you drew earlier. Add a horn.

5 Fill in Unicorn's hooves. Draw Unicorn's face. Add stripes to the horn and mane. Then add stars and a magic rainbow!

6 Color in your drawing!

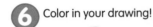

WHAT'S YOUR STORY?

Unicorn and Yeti build a forest out of shapes.
Imagine **you** are building it with them.
What would you add to the forest?
What shapes would you use? Write and draw your story!

scholastic.com/acorn